This book is for:

_____

from:

_____

Dedication

For my son, Benjamin.

Published by B&H Publishing Group, Nashville, Tennessee
All rights reserved.
Published in partnership with Brentwood Studios, Franklin, TN.
ISBN: 978-1-5359-3972-0
Scripture quotations are taken from the Holy Bible,
New International Version®, NIV® Copyright ©1973, 1978, 1984,
2011 by Biblica, Inc. Used by permission. All rights reserved worldwide.
Printed in Shenzhen, Guangdong, China in January 2019
1 2 3 4 5 • 23 22 21 20 19

A SLUGS & BUGS STORY

Who Will Play with Me?

RANDALL GOODGAME
illustrated by Cory Jones

B&H
kids
Nashville TN

Once upon a hillside,
Doug the slug came out to play.

Doug loves having fun.

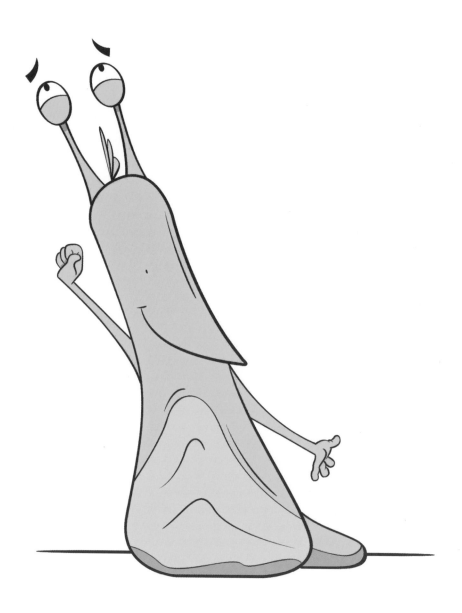

(He tries to have
some every day.)

With a push,

and then a squoosh,

the slug began to slide,

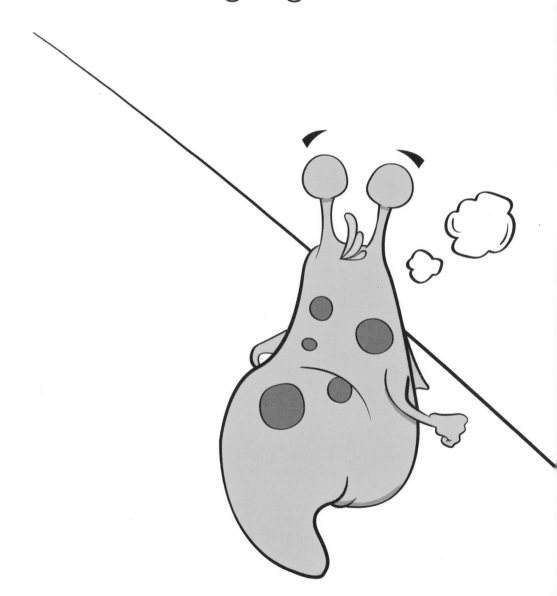

Climbing uphill
   toward the playground
      on the other side.

Slurshy sloggy
past two froggies
in a muddy dance,

Doug was smiling to himself, "I'm glad slugs don't wear pants!"

Doug kept chugging, slugging
toward the hilltop—

go Doug go!

(The hill was very small,
but Doug is very, *very* ...
well ...
not fast.)

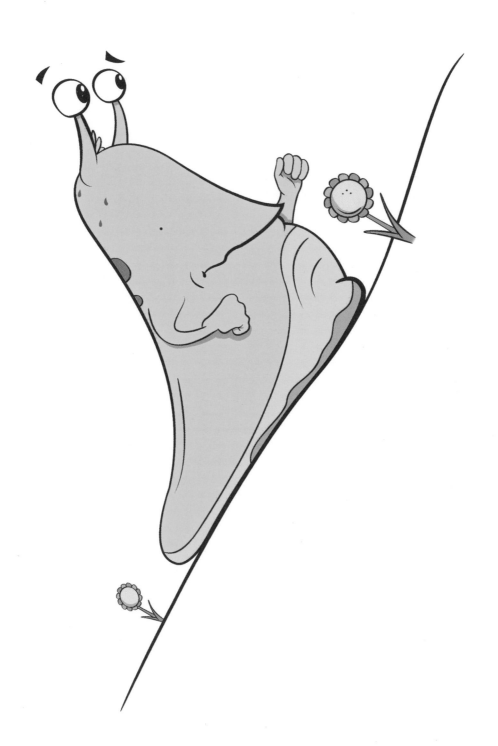

When he topped the hill,
he stopped to take a look around.

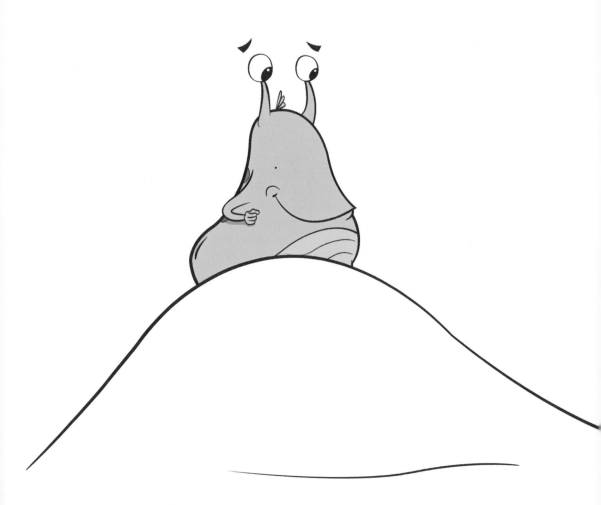

That's when he saw

the wagon . . .

all alone and upside down.

Just imagine—a red wagon!
Green and yellow too!
Tumped over in the grass,
still cool and wet
with morning dew.

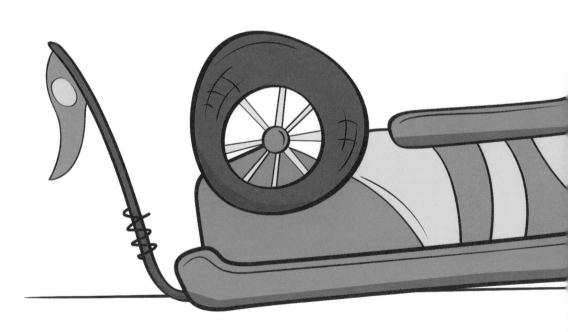

He took one side
and lifted up

and pushed

and pushed,

almost got stuck.

Then one more push with
all his might,
and with a *CRASH*
   it fell upright.

If you think Doug climbed in,

"I want to ride,"
Doug softly said.

"I want to ride."
He scratched his head.

"I WANT TO RIDE

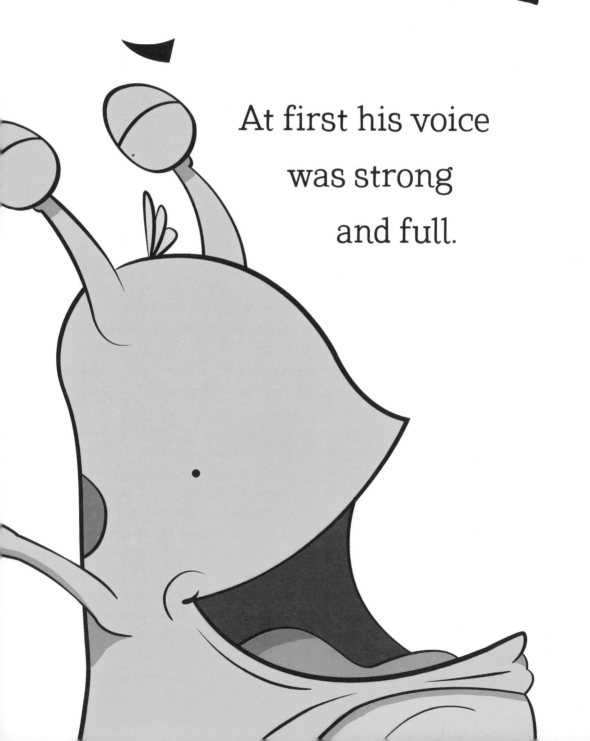

At first his voice
was strong
and full.

IN THE WAGON!"

"I want to ride in the wagon,
but I need someone to pull."

Who will play with me?
Doug thought
    and thought
        and thought some more.

And then he thought
    a thought
        that he had never
            thought before.

He took a breath
and slid up straight,
his slug-mouth open wide,
and hollered to
the neighborhood,

"WHO WANTS A WAGON RIDE?"

"I do!" came a friendly voice,
a flitter, and a smile.

And there was Doug's
friend Sparky with his
super Sparky style!

"Sparky! What a fun surprise!
Hop in, and hold on tight!"

So Sparky did.
 He sat, crouched low,
  and waited to take flight.

He closed one eye.

He gripped the sides;

they felt warm from the sun.

Still waiting, he heard

Doug call out, "Woohooo!

This is so fun!"

"You can start pulling!" Sparky called. "I *am* pulling!" said Doug.

"I heard some . . . squirching," Sparky said, "but barely felt a tug."

Like a melting snowman,
Doug's face fell,
and he said, "Oh."

"I thought I was going fast,
but I'm a slug ...
and slugs *are* slow."

Then all the fun began to thaw,
and Doug felt like a big fat flaw.
He cried a tear that no one saw.

Then Sparky started thinking
in his lightning-buggy brain,
And also in his heart
('cause sometimes those things
are the same).

He fluttered down to hug his friend
and think a moment more.
Then Sparky thought
    a thought
        much like
            the thought
                Doug thought before.

WAAAAHOOOOOOO!!!!!

Of course! They swapped, and finally, Doug got his wagon ride.

They whooped
and hooped and
loop-dee-looped,

with smiles
a mile wide.

Doug called out,
"To the swingset!"
and he slunk up on a swing.

But wagon-pulling
had worn out poor Sparky,
wing-to-wing.

Sparky tried to lightning push,
but his limbs were lightning mush,

He fell on his lightning tush.
(Fpfpffbbbt!)

First there was a giggle,
then a gaffy-laughing burst,

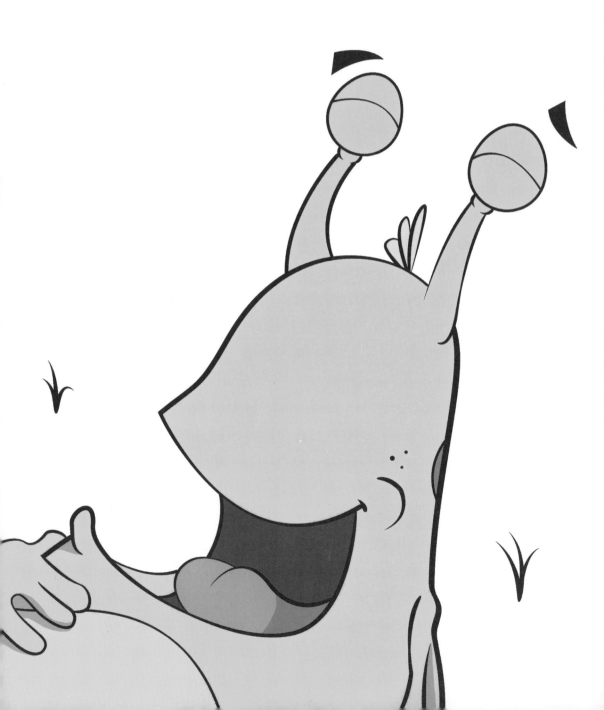

That kind of gaffy-laughter
that can never be reversed.

And after all their chuckle-snorts
and wheezy-grins were through,

Doug thought of his friend Sparky . . .

and he knew just what to do.

In humility, value others
above yourselves.
—Philippians 2:3